Big Girls Don't Cry -
Until They Do
A Novel
ENGINEER
SUPERVISOR
KJ
I0769223

NOVEL TITLES BY RENEE GOODWIN

A Love, A Life, Forgone

Living Past Shadows

GG LIFE LESSON STORYBOOK SERIES ®
BY RENEE GOODWIN

GG Cleans House – Learning Teamwork

GG Meets Her Match – Becoming Forever Friends

GG Asks, "Is Jesus In Your Class?" – Seek, Know, Guide,

Inspire

GG Takes Action – Practicing Health Safety

GG Sets Sail – Seeing the Beauty of the World

GG Works The Honeybees – Helping Nature

Big Girls Don't Cry – Until They Do

Renee Goodwin

GOODWIN GLOBAL PUBLISHING, LLC
TYLER, TEXAS

DEDICATION

To engineers blazing trails and pioneering paths for others
to follow.

BIG GIRLS DON'T CRY –
UNTIL THEY DO

PART ONE

Looking back, I am astounded how a *modest decision*, a *brief encounter*, and a *slight action* can change one's life. Yet, it happened to me. I was a recent petroleum engineering graduate of a very prestigious university. Having buried my life in textbooks for several years, I managed to acquire a high-grade point average allowing me to choose from multiple career opportunities. Unlike most of my fellow petroleum engineering graduates who chose to begin their careers as reservoir engineers, with much deliberation, I chose to begin my career path as an offshore drilling engineer. *Hence, my modest decision.* My thinking at the time, working as a drilling engineer (offshore and onshore) then switching to production engineering to lastly progress to reservoir engineering would make me a well-rounded petroleum engineer. Then to finalize my master plan, with all said and done, engineering wise, I would be fully equipped to establish my own oil and gas corporation.

So, off I go into the vast waters of the Gulf of Mexico only to realize years later, I was the first woman offshore drilling engineer supervisor for a major oil corporation pioneering these waters. The days were long, spending twenty hours of a twenty-four-hour day awake, working. Similar to the many waking hours spent during my college years studying. I don't realize it at the time, but I came to know my college years saved me in many ways. I was conditioned to stay awake for long periods of time and still have my cognitive senses about me. The hours spent in the classroom taking notes from highly qualified professors of the oil and gas industry prepared me for the work at hand. My knowledge gained from my alma mater was put to the test immediately as I stepped off the helicopter transporting me to the offshore drilling rig, my new home for the next seven days. My work schedule was called a triple seven. I worked offshore seven days, I was off duty seven days, then I worked in the office seven days. It was a rigorous

lifestyle but greatly appreciated in my years to come.

* * *

I was the youngest child expected to be tough like my older two brothers, Doug and Scott.

My brothers would tease me constantly. In today's society it would be considered bullying. However, when bullying happens within your family, it is passed off as sibling rivalry. Why? I don't know. From my perspective, there was no sibling rivalry or jealousy. I did not aspire to be anything remotely resembling my brothers' looks, intellect, mannerisms, nothing.

Every day Doug and Scott would make fun of me. One day they would tease me about my hair. My hair was very curly. Doug would shout to Scott, "Katie put her finger in a light socket." They both would laugh. I didn't say a word.

On another day, they would call me "Squirt" because I was short for my age. They would taunt saying, "Katie needs stilts to be able to see above the cabinet." They both would laugh. I didn't say a word.

A day didn't go by without both of them telling me that I need to scrub my face harder to get all of the brown spots off. My brothers were rudely referring to my freckles. Unfortunately for me, I spent most of a day outside in the sun causing my face to be covered in freckles.

I tried to correct these flaws as I was made to believe I had by straightening my hair, wearing hats to cover my face and my freckles, putting socks in my shoes to make me taller, and on and on.

Nothing I did stopped the teasing. I was very unhappy. I just wanted to cry. But, day after day, I was told repeatedly by every member of my family, "Big Girls Don't Cry." This statement was drilled into me, "Big Girls Don't Cry." But I was a little girl. I wanted to cry. I wanted to release my hurts and sadness. Unfortunately, for me, I kept all my sufferings bottled up deep within.

After years of denying my feelings, any feelings, good or bad, happy or sad, I knew I was reaching a breaking point. Something had to change. Lucky for me, it did. I went to college. For the first time in my life, I was in a new environment, surrounded by people wanting to get to know me, for me. Actually, it was the first time in my life I was able to learn about myself.

* * *

It is my first day of college life. So far, so good. I meet my roommate, Mary. Mary is from a small town and is an only child. I met Mary's parents, briefly. They seemed to be very loving people. Mary's father was a veterinarian specializing in the care of large animals. Mary came to college to study veterinarian medicine. However, being about my size, Mary said she wants to share her father's animal clinic but care for small animals. Wow, I thought. Mary has her career all planned.

I had no idea what I should study, needed to study or

what I wanted to be. I knew I enjoyed mathematics and science. I thought maybe I could start there. I was fortunate to be the salutatorian of my high school graduating class. I really thought I was the valedictorian. I had a 4.0 grade point average. However, the day before graduation, I was preparing my valedictorian speech and the principal called me to his office saying there had been a calculation error and Robert Butler was the valedictorian so I would be the salutatorian. As the tears start welling in my eyes, immediately in the back of my mind I hear, "Big Girls Don't Cry." In my heart, in my being, I push my disappointment, my hopes, my dreams into my internal abyss.

* * *

I arrived at my first college classroom. I peruse the room. I call it a room but it was really equivalent to a conference hall. I am guessing there were two hundred students milling around trying to find a seat. I thought it best not to sit too close to the front but I wanted to make sure I could see the professor and the notes on the board so I chose to sit in the middle of the fifth row of the more than fifty rows to choose from.

A few minutes later a group of girls took the seats to my left. Right before class began, a guy rushed in and took the seat to my right. I tried to size him up looking out of the corner of my eye. From what I could decipher, he appeared to be an average joe, brown hair, brown eyes, dressed in khakis and a polo shirt. Not bad. As the professor called the roll, I learned his name was Brian Johnson. I hope he was listening when the professor called my name, Katie Thomas.

The class time flew by it seemed. I was constantly taking notes. When the professor dismissed the class, I wanted to introduce myself to Brian but I had less that ten minutes to walk across campus to my next class. At this moment, I wished I had planned my schedule with more time in between classes. My class with Brian met only once a week so maybe I will see him next week.

I wonder if Brian will sit by me again.?

* * *

Brian did sit by me at our next class meeting. We became good friends and great study partners. I believe the one most important thing I learned during my four years of college is to make sure I had a good study partner in every class. I was also fortunate to have an experienced college counselor. With my high school achievements in math and chemistry, she suggested I study engineering. Even though I was studying petroleum engineering and Brian was studying mechanical engineering, there were many courses both curriculums shared. So, Brian and I made sure each semester we signed up for at least one class together.

As time went on, Brian and I realized we truly enjoyed each other's company. I guess you could say we were "college sweethearts." During study breaks, we would get coffee, maybe coffee and dessert. On weekends, we would go to dinner and possibly a movie depending if there was still money in the money jar or not. Brian didn't worry about his money jar very much. Brian's father owned a well-established engineering firm. The firm employed over one hundred employees of which Brian would be one someday. Brian had an education fund that financed his college expenses. I earned several academic scholarships during my high school years that helped pay my college expenses. With these monies plus working odd jobs on campus, I was able to pay my way through college one semester at a time. It worked.

During finals week, when the money jar was almost empty, I would study, take the exam then sell the book back to the campus bookstore. Then, I would have money to buy a sandwich. I repeated this maneuver throughout the week one exam at a time. I knew I had to "feed my brain" to finish strong. This plan worked well enough throughout the years.

Most weeks the nights were spent studying for exams or working on papers and projects. Once all were completed, Brian and I would go country western dancing. We would dance the "Cotton-Eye Joe," line dance to Alan Jackson's "Good Time," and waltz to George Strait's "You Look So Good in Love." But, the best part of the evening, happens when we slow dance to Etta James' "At Last" because I know Brian will kiss me as the song ends.

Sometimes, Brian would surprise me inviting me for a fancy dinner. He would come to my door to pick me up with roses in hand. For such occasions, Brian always chose a different restaurant so I was always surprised. Brian called ahead and pre-ordered our meals starting with appetizers and most importantly included desserts. The waitstaff gave us their undivided attention the entire evening. Yes, Brian swept me off my feet!

The four years of college seemed to fly by. As graduation neared, Brian decided to enroll into the school's MBA program. He felt with engineering and business degrees, he would be more of an asset in his family's engineering firm. I was happy for Brian but sad

for our relationship. We told each other we would write

every day, alternate traveling to be with each other on

weekends and vacation together during the holidays. I

lived the experience to say, "Absence does make the heart

grow fonder. However, distance is taxing on a

relationship." As Brian's studies became more time

consuming and my offshore work schedule changed

constantly due to matters out of my control, Brain and I

saw less and less of each other.

The day came we both were dreading but knew

for each other was the right thing to do, "Break-Up." I

had a few days off so I met Brian at his apartment. We

enjoyed our days together reminiscing of our college

years. We made a beautiful couple. We never expressed

it out loud, but we always thought that one day we would

start our own engineering company.

At that moment, I had to realize, somethings are

not meant to be. We hugged, we kissed, we said

goodbye. Then, I returned to the Gulf of Mexico. During my journey back, I so wanted to cry. I lost the love of my life, my only love. A wonderful chapter of my life ended, yet I wanted it to continue. I so wanted to cry. I drove in pure silence yet hearing over and over again in my mind, the words, "Big Girls Don't Cry. Big Girls Don't Cry. Big Girls Don't Cry."

PART TWO

Not traveling during my spare time, as minimal as it was, now that Brian and I were no longer together, I had to force myself to look for ways to start my personal life again. At first, I admit, I tried to work overtime so I did not have to address this issue. Although, sooner or later, I knew I had to put myself into position to meet others. *Hence, my brief encounter.*

I noticed a job posting one day. The company needed an engineer to oversee repairs on an offshore oil rig while dry-docked. This seemed like a good opportunity to change my surroundings. I applied and shortly afterwards, I was re-assigned to a quaint city on the coastline. The re-assignment did not state the length of the job, only that I was to stay on location until the rig repairs were finished. I figured it was worth the gamble at this stage of my life.

Once I arrived, I realized the location housed oil rigs from various companies needing major repairs.

The bay was stacked with rigs, one beside another as far as you could see. I walked for miles it seemed until I came to my rig assignment, TA-652, a semi-submersible rig. I was amazed how much larger it appeared now dry-docked than when I was assigned to the rig several months before working as the company supervisor offshore drilling engineer.

Wow, now the work begins. I walked around and up and down the rig to familiarize myself. Before arriving, I reviewed the plans and specifications for all of the repairs. Being a woman in this male dominated field, I found my odds for success increased when I had all my bases covered, checked and re-checked before introducing myself as "the boss." Now, it was time to meet the rig foreman and the crew and review the work at hand as I walked with them around the rig again.

I left the rig close to sundown. On my way to find my home away from home, I found a small grocery store, picked up a few items and continued on my way. The company rented an efficiency apartment equipped with the necessary amenities just small in square footage compared to my apartment back home. Although, I admit, I quickly felt comfortable in my humble abode. I looked forward to being in a place where no one knew me. I could be me wearing my many hats; being me as an engineer with my hair pulled back wearing my company baseball cap, being me as the boss with my hair stuffed in my company hard hat, or be me on my days off letting my hair blow in the wind under my cowgirl hat.

Quickly, I got into a routine. Each weekday before 7:00 a.m. I reported to the rig and made my morning rounds with the rig foreman viewing the status of each repair in progress. Working a dry-dock shift was different than working an offshore drilling rig shift. Drilling offshore was a twenty-four hour a day, seven days a week operation hoping to stop the madness by reaching the oil/gas producing zone. Working on a dry-docked rig was only a five day a week schedule usually from sun up to sun down, dawn to dusk. Definitely, the dry-dock schedule allowed some time to relax on the weekends which I thoroughly enjoyed.

I continued my routine, every evening on my way back to my apartment, I would buy a few items at the little grocery store I found on my first day on the job. I thought since I had some time and to give more purpose to my assignment, I would try some new recipes and hone my cooking skills. I tried my hand at making chicken cordon bleu, beef wellington, lasagna, stir-fry and various casseroles. To keep from indulging in all of these calories adding unwanted and unneeded pounds, I packed to-go boxes to pass out to the rig crew. The surprise meals helped form a healthy working relationship with all, especially since I was the "woman boss" giving orders to a group of men.

I thought I might find other women engineers overseeing the dry-dock repairs on some of the other rigs, but I seemed to be the only woman engineer at the time.

It may sound exciting being the only woman but it can be rough and tough. Day in and day out overseeing the actions of over seventy men, all bigger and taller than myself – with huge egos – is challenging to say the least. At the end of the day however, my saving grace, the men all knew, I was "the boss." If they were disrespectful, argumentative or made inappropriate advances they knew they would be permanently "dry-docked." With this understanding, the job assignment progressed relatively smoothly.

***

A few weeks into the assignment, at the end of the day, I was making my evening grocery store stop. I had decided to make chicken fried steak, mashed potatoes and gravy. My idea of comfort food. I was feeling a little homesick. I thought some comfort food would cheer me up. To make the meal sound healthy at least, I added a green salad to my menu. However, my taste buds were contemplating brownies a la mode for dessert.

Scanning the refrigerated meat section for the perfect package of sirloin, as I reached in, to my surprise another hand landed on the sirloin at the same time. With an "EEEKKK," I jumped back still holding onto the meat. It was the last package of sirloin and I had my heart set on "my comfort food." But the other hand was still holding on to the package, too. As my eyes slowly gazed up, I viewed a very distinguished man, black hair with some grey around the temples, shocking blue eyes with a very masculine build. Even though he was undeniably handsome, I held my ground holding onto "my" beef cutlets. I was hoping he would let go first. *Yes, I know, a foolish thought.*

I hear a deep voice say, "It seems we have a predicament." Having just left the jobsite, still in my "boss" mode, I wanted to say, "There is no predicament. You just need to let go of the package and I will be on my way." Usually, to escape my "boss" mode required a hot bath and a few sips of wine. Luckily, I caught myself.

Looking into his awesome blue eyes, I knew he meant no harm. I reply, "I have my taste buds primed for steak tonight. What is on your menu?"

"The same. However, if you agree, I will ask the butcher to split the package. I am only cooking for one so that should leave plenty for your dinner plans."

This is my chance to let him know, it is just me. Should I speak up? "I am just cooking for one, also." *Yikes, was I too forthcoming with such information? Well, it is too late. The words are out there now.*

Mr. Blue Eyes responds, "I am happy to invite you to share my meal, but I don't want to be too forward."

Shaking my head breaking the spell I was under, coming back to my senses, I kindly say, "I appreciate your offer. Let's just split the package." *Oh, was I too bossy?*

The butcher handed us the packages. I headed directly to the check-out counter. My mystery man disappeared down another aisle.

My meal was delicious. I seasoned and battered the meat to perfection. The secret is to put all of your flour and seasonings in a paper bag, shake, shake, shake so that the meat is covered thoroughly with batter. The mashed potatoes were creamy. I surprised myself, my gravy was not lumpy. Yea! As I savored each bite, I wondered how the meal might have been if I had shared my dinner with my mystery man.

Later that week, I was sitting on a bench by the docks watching the sunset. My wonderment of the beautiful colors illuminating from the sun disappearing quickly below the horizon was suddenly interrupted as I spied my mystery man approaching. I forced myself to look straight ahead pretending I didn't see him. I noticed my palms were sweaty as I began to wring my hands. *Relax, Katie, relax.*

"Well, we meet again," my mystery man announces.

"I suppose so."

"What is on the menu tonight?" he asks.

"I am not sure."

"I was thinking pizza. I found an authentic pizzeria nearby. As he blinks his big blue eyes my way he asks, "Would you like to join me?"

I hesitate.

"It is within walking distance," he adds as his eyes continue to mesmerize me.

My stomach gives a growl hearing the mention of pizza, one of my favorite foods. "Sounds like a delicious idea. I'm in."

"Perfect!"

As we begin walking down the dock he says, "By the way, my name is Roger." My brief encounter now becomes a budding romance.

***

Come to find out, Roger was the rig foreman for a major oil and gas corporation. I was happy to know that Roger worked for a different company than mine. Otherwise, if we worked for the same company, I would have been Roger's boss. Such an arrangement I don't think creates the foundation for a healthy relationship.

Roger invited me to join him for lunch the next day. As we talked, we realized we had many commonalities. Our conversations flowed with ease.

I begin with, "In my solitude, I enjoy playing the guitar."

"Me, too. In fact, I have written a few songs."

"I have written songs, also. But I struggle with the melodies."

"Maybe I can help you with that. Do you have your guitar with you?"

"I try not to go anywhere without it."

"Would you like to come over to my house Friday night for dinner? If you want, please bring your song lyrics and guitar and we can work on some melodies."

"If you promise not to be judgmental. I use

songwriting as a means to vent any troubles, frustrations, disappointments and worries in my life."

"Do your songs ever reflect your joy and happiness?

That question stopped me in my tracks. Did I just become transparent? Have I been living my life from one disappointment to another? Moment to moment just waiting for the sky to fall in on me or another shoe to drop. Do I have happiness in my life? Yikes! Does he see me as totally pathetic? Now what? I need a huge comeback statement.

My comeback, "If, I happen to be sad, I write songs to help me feel so I can heal and move on!"

I hope that sounded positive enough. I need to change the subject of conversation.

"Friday night should work. What time? Can I bring something for the meal?"

And maybe I can conveniently forget my guitar!

"Can you come about 7:00? The local market

advertised fresh fish available Friday. If it is agreeable with you, we can have a fish fry."

"Sounds great. I will bring my famous "hush puppies" and a surprise dessert."

Speaking of dessert, we both looked at our watches realizing we had lost track of time. We asked the waitress for separate checks, paid, tipped and back to work we went in opposite directions. As I walk back to the docked rig, I start to panic wondering what have I got myself into now. Singing, songwriting, playing the guitar in front of someone else, in reality, a stranger. *Oh my!*

The next few days seem to fly by and now it is Friday. After work, I mixed, battered and fried the hush puppies to perfection, a golden brown. I decided on the way to Roger's, I would stop by the grocery store and buy fudge sundae supplies to make for dessert. Now, all dressed in my blue jeans, floral shirt and sandals, I debate whether to conveniently forget my guitar and lyrics. Yes? No? Yes/No? Yes/No/Maybe? Before I made myself crazy, I grabbed my song sheet and guitar and out the door I went.

The meal was delicious. My hush puppies complimented Roger's perfectly seasoned fried catfish. We were stuffed but continued forward with assembling our fudge sundaes which were also, over the top delicious.

Roger suggests, "My guitar is in the living room. Let's take a peek at your song lyrics." Now all along I was hoping he would forget about the song so I left my guitar in my car. Seeing no way out of this song session, I respond, "My guitar is in my car. I'll go get it." I confess, as I approached my car, I contemplated a quick escape. Knowing I would not be able to dodge Roger since we were working at the same shipyard, I decided to face my fate.

I walk in with my guitar and song sheet. Roger is on the couch strumming a nice melody. His guitar is beautiful, made by Fender. I asked him where he got his guitar. He said his grandfather gave it to him. Apparently, his grandfather had been in the music business for years. I opened my guitar case, pulled out my Yamaha. My guitar was an older model as well. I bought it with my birthday money I got when I turned sixteen. It was beautiful in its own right. Plus, it was a smaller guitar that fit me perfectly making it easier to strum.

The rest of the evening flew by as we knocked around a few melodies to a little song I wrote dreaming of a childhood I always hoped to live, "Puttin' On My Cowboy Boots." The melodies we played were fun and simple. It was a nice way to spend an evening together.

Our romance blossomed during the next few weeks as Roger and I were able to spend special moments together. We casually spent our weeknights cooking meals for each other. We would cuddle on the couch, share sweet kisses with each other and talk about our future plans. My heart melted each time I looked into his enchanting blue eyes. I wondered how he felt as he looked into my deep brown eyes. Could he see my eyes expressing my love, now and forever?

During our date nights to the pizzeria, we would hold hands walking down the street window shopping. One night we passed a jewelry store showcasing engagement rings. Roger pointed to a beautiful sapphire and diamond ring saying, "Let me see your hand. Yes, I do believe that ring is perfect for you."

As I lay in bed, I think I am in shock. Roger showing me engagement rings. Is he going to pop the question? He really does love me. Wait! Am I ready to hear his words, "Katie, I know we have only known each other for a short while. But I fell in love with you the night you had the butcher split the package of sirloin at the grocery store. Katie, I love every ounce of you. I truly adore you. I want to be your forever companion. Will you marry me?" Oh my! Do I have an answer to the question? I know I love Roger. In fact, I don't want to spend a moment without him. Marriage for us? Can it happen? Will it be forever?

***

One morning the rig foreman announced the last maintenance work on the rig was completed so that completed my work as well. I was expected back at the office the next day. Roger had some unexpected complications arise on his rig workover that day causing him to work into the early morning. Having packed my things that night, the next morning I left Roger a note on his door as I started my eight-hour drive back home. My note to Roger said:

Roger:

What a wonderful surprise for me
to have met you. I truly have enjoyed our
time together these past few months. I
never expected my work to help me cross
paths with someone as special as you. I
am overjoyed with excitement of how our
love may grow with time. Even though
our homes are miles apart, I think we both
feel our love can withstand knowing we

both will travel that extra mile to be together. I know we can do it. In my heart, I feel we belong together. We make a perfect team, in our work and in our play.

I wrote my address and phone number on the back of the note and added, "Let me know as soon as you have time and we can meet again."

Love you all the world,
Katie

***

The weeks, the months went by and no calls, no letters from Roger. Over and over in my mind, all I could think was, "Oh Katie, what a fool you are." I told myself, "You should have known he was a company man through and through. He just used your goodness to make his days and nights a little more interesting." And to think I really felt he was going to ask me to marry him. How I don't want to face this reality, another failed relationship. And oh, how I want to cry away all of my sadness, my hurt, my disappointment, my loss. But I just stay bottled up inside. All I can hear over and over again in the recesses of my mind, are the words, "Big Girls Don't Cry. Big Girls Don't Cry. Big Girls Don't Cry."

***

Several years later, I was closing out my seven days working offshore. It had been an exciting yet strenuous week. We had drilled to the target zone and yes there was oil. So much happens before, during and after an offshore drilling operation but then to hit "pay dirt" so to speak, it all seems to be worthwhile.

The helicopter was flying me back to shore. The pilot had the radio playing country music which I thought was strange but I was enjoying the tunes until I hear the disc jockey announce a new hit song, "Puttin' On My Cowboy Boots." My heart skipped several beats. I yell,

"What?" I startled the pilot and the helicopter took a dive for the water. He pulled back the throttle and quickly regained altitude while giving me a "what in the world is wrong with you" look. I apologized and tried to keep myself steady the remainder of the ride.

When I got home, I ran to my computer to look-up information about this "new hit song." As I read the song's review, my heart sank, my body crumbled to the floor. I only had to read the first line and I knew; my song had been stolen. My little wishful childhood song was now being sung by a popular country music singer. What hurt the most was reading "Lyrics and Melody by Roger Ellis." Hum, I never knew his last name. Now, I definitely wish I had never known his first name.

Another pitfall in my life. Just when I think I am healed and can go forward, I get thrown back into the dungeon. Darkness and gloom overwhelm me. I can't decide if I am more sad than angry or more angry than sad. Bottom line, I was in a bad place. Crying those tears, I needed to cry would have been a start to my healing. But it didn't happen, it couldn't happen. "Big Girls Don't Cry."

PART THREE

The company moved me from offshore drilling to onshore drilling. A short while later I was transferred to production engineering followed by reservoir engineering. I was working on a reservoir project one afternoon in the company library and a very handsome man wearing a suit and tie sat at the table beside me. He seemed to be looking up the same oil and gas data I was researching. *Hence, my slight action.* I offer him a book and ask, "Do you need this oil and gas data from 1990? I am finished using it." He replied, "That would be very helpful. Thank you."

As I handed him the book, I noticed he had monogrammed initials on his French cuffs, "TLB." I admit my curiosity was getting the best of me. I wanted to ask his name but I saved myself from possible embarrassment.

When I got back to my office, I took out the company directory. In the list of "Bs" I found one person with initials T and L. Could he be Thaddeus Lee Baxter, III? I admit, he looked like a Thaddeus Lee Baxter, III. In parenthesis by his name it said, (Thad). I agree, in the workplace, using the name Thad would work best.

Later that week I was scheduled to attend a meeting in a very large board room. As I arrived, as I always do, I quickly scanned each face. I knew most of the faces so I relaxed slightly then I see Parenthesis Thad. Again, dressed in suit and tie, French cuffed sleeves and gold stud cuff links. I took a seat at the opposite end of the table.

The meeting was long but durable. As I rose to leave, I hear, "Weren't you the kind lady that offered me a book the other day in the library? I apologize for not introducing myself earlier. My name is Thad." Now, I am thinking you are sharing the short version of your name. But I decided to play along saying, "That is nice of you to say. I hope the book was useful." Parenthesis Thad replied, "Yes, it contained the data I had been looking for. Seeing you again today, it seems we are both working on the same project." Keeping my distance, not to be too chummy, I respond, "Yes, it appears that we are." Parenthesis Thad says, "I look forward to future meetings. See you then." As I tried to say the same, he disappeared around the corner.

The next project meeting was held at a five-star restaurant downtown. My company was trying to persuade a client to sell their working interest in the project area. Usually wining and dining helps in these situations. I was happy I was not the lead engineer. I could stay focused yet relax and enjoy my evening. As I take my seat, I look up and in walks Parenthesis Thad. I admit the suits he wears to the office are very nice but the suit he is wearing this night must be a designer brand and he is wearing it well. With his tall, trim frame, wearing this pinstripe navy jacket, light blue button-down collared shirt and paisley tie with coordinating pocket square caused me to do a "double take." I had not noticed before but his hazel-colored eyes compliment his wavy dark brown hair.

So as not to stare, I looked down fidgeting with my napkin and silverware. Well, my thought of a relaxing evening was a fleeting memory as Parenthesis Thad took the seat beside me. I felt ill at ease from the get go. But, after a few glasses of wine which I usually do not drink at company functions, my nerves settled and I found conversing with Parenthesis Thad was enjoyable and amusing. Surprisingly, he has a great personality. Just looking at him, one would never have known.

At the end of the evening, as everyone began to depart, Parenthesis Thad says, "It was a very enjoyable evening. Visiting with you definitely was the highlight." I reply, "It was a very nice evening. I appreciated visiting with you also." He suggests, "Maybe next week, we can meet for lunch or dinner." I look at him strangely and he quickly says, "So we can discuss this project in more detail." Hearing those words, I settle a minute. The last thing I want to do is have a personal relationship with a

co-worker. I have never known such relationships to end

well. I respond saying, "I agree. This project needs a lot

of attention. I guess I will see you at the office. Good-

night." Parenthesis Thad bids me goodnight as he joins a

group of other co-workers as they exit the restaurant.

As I drive home, I replay the events of the

evening in my mind. I admit I did enjoy Parenthesis

Thad's company. It seemed we had common

interests other than work related subjects. But, why am

I even thinking of this topic? I can't get involved with a

co-worker, no matter how handsome, well-dressed,

debonaire … he may be.

***

So, I didn't listen to my inner self telling me

to keep my relationship with Parenthesis Thad strictly

professional. A few weeks later, we met for lunch, and

dinner. Then, dinner and lunch. Before I realized it,

Parenthesis Thad and I were a couple. In fact, I refer to

him as just "Thad" now. He never knew I looked him up in the company directory and since had been calling him Parenthesis Thad. I will keep that my little secret.

Thad and I share a remarkable relationship. We see each other off and on during the working day, usually sharing lunch. Then we always have dinner together at my home or his. On the weekends we visit the museums, maybe catch a matinee at the theater. The town has beautiful flower gardens we stroll through then pick a spot by the lake and have a picnic.

On rainy weekends, we stay snug in the house reading books, watching movies, listening to music and dancing. Of course, you would expect Thaddeus Lee Baxter, III to be an expert ball room dancer. As we dance, Thad twirls me around and around. He definitely makes me look like a much better dancer than I am. I feel like Cinderella at the Palace Ball as we waltz around the living room. Being with Thad feels like I am living in Wonderland.

I have to say, Thad is such a gentleman which I truly enjoy. He opens the car door for me. He lets me go first in line. Thad always helps me with my jackets. Yes, Thad is an all-around champion in my mind. I am head over heels for him. *Is he head over heels for me? I think he is. Is he just being a gentleman or does he share these thoughtful gestures because I am the love of his life and he treasures me being in his life?*

It was nearing the holiday season. Thad and I had vacation days to use or loose. That is how it works in the oil and gas world. Thad asked if I would like to spend a few days at his family home visiting his parents. Hmm. I pause. Thad is basically asking me to meet his parents, a Thaddeus Lee Baxter, Jr. and a Mrs. Thaddeus Lee Baxter, Jr. *Note to self: I need to ask Thad what is his mother's first name.*

Thad clears his throat getting my attention. I stammer a moment but so as not to hurt his feelings, I reply, "Yes that sounds like a great idea." Thad smiles, claps his hands with excitement and says, "I will call them now to let them know to expect us tomorrow." Suddenly, I felt I needed a crash course in etiquette from Emily Post. My head was swimming with so many questions: Will they like me? What if they don't like me? Will I fit in? What if there are ten pieces of dinnerware at my place setting for dinner? Will I know which fork to use? *And this is supposed to be my vacation.*

***

I admit, at first, sharing time with Thad's parents was stressful and at times personally overwhelming. I am not used to a high society lifestyle and that is exactly the lifestyle Thad is accustomed to. I respect the different lifestyles Thad and I were raised in. Anytime, life can be easier, I am all for it. I give Thad credit, though. He has the ability to make himself feel comfortable no matter the circumstance. I know I don't have that ability. If I find a situation uncomfortable, my facial expressions will undeniably show the angst. However, I give myself a little credit. When I am comfortable, I do relax and enjoy the time at hand. I do appreciate life's loving moments.

I had always lectured myself, no matter what, do not have a relationship with a co-worker. I still feel for my sake, this is good advice. However, my relationship with Thad, even though we are co-workers, to my surprise, we have been able to stay professional at work and loving at home. *What a relief.*

One Saturday night, Thad says, "Let's put on the Ritz, tonight." Looking puzzled and slightly apprehensive, I ask, "What are you suggesting?" He says, "Let's have a private Black-Tie Affair. I will put on my tux; I know you have a beautiful red evening gown I have been waiting to feast my eyes on you wearing and we will go "Out On The Town." I slowly respond, "Sounds exciting!" *I know what red evening gown he is referring to. The question is, can I fit into or not? Will I live up to these hungry eyes?*

A few hours later, we are off. Although the dress was a little snug here and there, I felt amazing. Thad was over the top handsome. Yes, he swept me off my feet yet, again. We had a wonderful evening, dinner and dancing like couples used to do in the 1950s. Thad, of course, was a gentleman through and through. I believe our ballroom dancing that night escalated to a new level.

Thad ordered Bananas Foster for two for dessert. While I was captivated watching the flames accentuate the glamour of our dessert, Thad poured our flutes of champagne. We toasted each other and dove into decadence. As I took a sip of champagne, I noticed something in the bottom of my glass. At such an up-scale restaurant, I didn't want to complain about a dirty glass. I gently set my glass off to the side. In doing so, I thought I saw a sparkle. Looking again I saw more than one sparkle. The glass was beaming with a rainbow of colors. Oh my gosh! There is a ring at the bottom of my glass. I gasped!

Thad moved in front of me and knelt down on one knee as he pulled a little black, velvet box from his coat pocket with the word "Tiffany on the front. Thad began pouring out his heart to me saying every word a girl wants to hear, "Katie, you are the most beautiful, intelligent, awesome woman I have ever known. I love you, adore you, respect you. I don't want to spend a moment away from you. Will you complete my dreams and make me the happiest man on earth? Will you marry me?" He opens the little black box showing the most gorgeous ring I have ever seen. There were more diamonds than I could count. I was totally taken by surprise. *Why was I worried about the ring in the bottom of my champagne glass? Is Thad double proposing?*

I feel Thad anxiously waiting for me to say "Yes!" I was anxiously waiting for me to say "Yes!" My heart melted as I looked into his hazel brown eyes and gazed at his handsome face. Taking a deep breath, I blurt out, "Yes, yes, I would love to be your wife!" Thad took my hand and slipped the ring on my finger. A perfect fit.

Thad and I enjoyed our engagement time. Both our families, friends and co-workers were so happy for us. I was beginning my "Happily Ever After" life. A life I really never expected for myself but a life I am thankful to be living.

***

Unlike me, I was suddenly interested in wedding planning. In my spare time, I browsed bridal magazines and wedding venue ads. I discovered my favorite flowers are white roses. I have always known my favorite cake is chocolate with strawberry filling and chocolate fudge frosting. Realizing though, my chocolate cake will have to sub as the Groom's cake. All well and good because Thad's favorite cake is Italian Cream with extra coconut and pecans. So, Thad's Italian Cream will be the Bride's Cake. It works for me.

My wedding ideas and planning quickly came to halt. Thad announced that his parents had secured their local country club for the wedding thereby choosing a Saturday in June date. The country club had a special patio used for wedding ceremonies and the sit down dinner including cakes, drinks and all flower arrangements were included. Basically, all Thad and I had to do was "show up."

It is fair to say, at first, I was disappointed. Then, I realized the headaches I was spared. My disappointments quickly took an about face. Now, I could concentrate on me, the bride and my bridal gown. I pictured me in my mind's eye on my wedding day. I could see joy, love, excitement, and endless blessings. *And white roses?*

***

A few days into the month of May, our office called a worldwide meeting. All personnel within the company had to sign in for the meeting however available, in person, via satellite, third party phone call… As I entered the meeting room, there was standing room only. I spied Thad standing along the opposite wall. The company executive officer welcomed everyone then began announcing new job assignments. My department was to remain as is. However, Thad's department was being dismantled. All personnel in that department were being re-assigned to the company office in Alaska. I am in shock as I look across the room at Thad. It seems he can't even move. This announcement truly blindsided both of us. The executive re-assured everyone that the new arrangements were best for all and for the company. The executive stated those moving would receive specific directions in a forthcoming email. My heart sank. I can't believe what is happening. *What are we going to do?*

Thad and I were not able to get to one another. He sent me a text suggesting we meet at our favorite restaurant at 7:00. I counted the minutes. When I arrived, Thad was seated at our special table. We kissed and hugged feeling both shaking within. Thad had ordered wine so we talked and sipped and sipped and talked for several hours. I thought one could not be blindsided twice in one day. But it happened and it happened to me.

Thad received the company email explaining his new assignment was a giant promotion. He was to be the top executive engineer for the Alaska office. He would oversee all operations including drilling, production, reservoir and a special pipeline project. The email instructed all personnel were to report in 30 days. *But our wedding was in 45 days.*

Thad shared it was a promotion of a lifetime. He was excited to get started. As he witnessed the look on my face, he stopped speaking mid-sentence then manages to say, "Oh!"

"I apologize Katie. I am sorry I forgot myself."

"What about us?"

"We can both go to Alaska together. You can resign from your position here. I am sure you can find another job in Alaska."

"What about our wedding?"

"I am sure my parents had a back-up plan. The country club will reimburse any expenditures."

"At a time like this, your concern is your parents' reimbursements."

"I didn't mean it the way it sounded."

"Sure, you did!"

"Katie, please."

"Please what?" Please understand that your career is more important than mine. Please understand that you do love me but this promotion means the world to you. Please understand that you want to be free from your commitment to love and cherish me." I took off the engagement ring, calmly placed it on the table and bid Thad farewell.

In 45 days, I am "To-Be-A-Bride." I picture me, wearing a beautiful white wedding gown with a long flowing train. My long brown hair pinned up with a braid of tiny white roses. I am carrying a full bouquet of large white roses entwined with long strands of green ivy and sprigs of baby breath. I can feel my excitement from my head to my toes. I am to be Mrs. Thaddeus Lee Baxter, III.

But now I am a "Nothing." I have reduced myself to being a "Zero." I used to be a very confident, independent, intelligent woman. Now, a "Nothing." Why Katie, why do you allow this to happen to you over and over again? I suppose all along I really am a very insecure, dependent, naive individual. *When everything seems so right, how can it go so wrong*? I beg myself, please let me cry. Please let me cry so I can release myself from this anguish. I beg, please let me cry. But all I can hear is myself reminding me, "Oh no Katie, "Big Girls Don't Cry," "Big Girls Don't Cry," "Big Girls Don't Cry.""

PART FOUR

I work day and night. My objective: to have experience in all three oil and gas engineering disciplines. True, but not the entire truth. My objective: to bury myself in my work as a means to forget my heartbreak, my sorrows from failed relationships. Not just Thad of recent but Roger and Brian, where I suppose this trail of failed relationships seemed to start.

Getting myself back on track, once I accomplish my engineering goals, I decide to take the leap of faith and establish my own oil and gas corporation. Hence, I become president and chief executive officer of KT Exploration, Inc. Using my initials for my company name seemed appropriate. Plus, it served a dual purpose. From the name, no one would know it was a female owned oil and gas corporation. Definitely, a plus in this specific industry.

Being honest with myself, I know there are no guarantees that my company will be successful no matter how hard I work. Not that I was viewing my glass half empty but knowing if my company didn't "make it," I would have to return to the major oil and gas corporation world. To do that, I would need a business degree. So, I worked the company during the day and went to school at night earning my master's degree in business administration.

Within five years, my company was able to drill, produce and operate several oil fields and turn a profit. From there, I felt the sky was the limit. It was hard work, yet I was happy staying busy. And earning my business degree during that time was a bonus in many regards.

To help businesses stay current with industry activities, a world-wide exposition is held yearly. This year, the exposition is scheduled close-by and I decided to attend. It is always a good idea to circulate amongst your peers at these gatherings. However, even though I am the president of an oil and gas corporation, I keep a low profile. I don't necessarily advertise my position.

As I am wondering around this enormous venue, rather anonymously, visiting with different industry service vendors, I look up and see Thad walking towards me. I don't think he sees me so I duck into one of the vendor booths as he walks by. Wow, Thad is here all the way from Alaska. It never dawned on me when I decided to come to the exposition that I would see anyone I knew, much less, my last heartbreak. Even though I only had a quick glance, Thad was still as handsome as ever. *Ugh!* As I dare to come out of the booth, it seems the coast is clear and I proceed to walk in the opposite direction of Thad.

The day proceeds and I am thankful I have not seen Thad again. The exposition is such a large event hosting thousands of people, I doubt if I will run into him again. I decide to venture to the section demonstrating new rig technology (offshore and onshore). The entire idea of drilling deep into the earth, sometimes navigating through hundreds of feet of water before entering the depths of the earth is quite astonishing. As

I am checking out the semi-submersible rig simulators, I

can't believe my eyes but there is Roger. Apparently, he

is still working for the same company and his

showing the audience the latest dynamic positioning

system improvements for semi-submersibles.

I think I was able to blend in with the crowd. I

don't think he saw me. I nonchalantly turn around and

head to another section. Again, I am overwhelmed.

What are the odds of me seeing not one old flame, but

two. *I should have stayed home.*

The exposition is a three-day event. As the first

day is nearing closing time, I head for the exit. I am

exhausted walking miles around the exposition, one

booth after another. Near the exit I see another section

of booths new to the exposition labeled "Business and

Finance". As I look through the list of vendors, I read,

"Johnson Engineering and Accounting". *Could this be

Brian's family's business?* I venture closer for a better

look and I see a picture of the company employees. I immediately spy Brian in the picture, his brown hair, brown eyes and dashing smile. But then I spy Brian in real life handing out flyers advertising Johnson Engineering and Accounting. I see Brian's name tag, "Brian Johnson, Sr. Accountant". *Wow, Brian didn't follow his engineering passion. He became an accountant.* I turn sharply and look for another exit.

***

That evening having a glass of wine and thoughts of Brian, Roger, and Thad rushing through my mind sends me back to what I call my "dark times." The memories with Brian as we studied together. Being "college sweethearts," our relationship was so fresh, so new, so exciting until it wasn't. Those feelings of my first love, feelings that will never be felt again suddenly vanish as if it all never happened. But my heart knows it did. *"Big Girls Don't Cry!"*

As I feel my emotions building inside of me,

going against my better judgement, I pour another glass of wine.

The memories with Roger as we worked together in an "out of the ordinary circumstance" allowed a special love to develop in a short amount of time with a greater love just waiting on the horizon. Waiting months and months yet that vista was never seen. Then the double crush, my song of childhood hopes was taken without permission and used for personal gains. I feel myself spiraling down again as if it all just happened yesterday. How could I have totally misjudged him? *"Big Girls Don't Cry!"*

Now, definitely against my better judgement, I pour wine glass number three as thoughts of Thad begin streaming through my mind.

Thaddeus Lee Baxter, III is every girl's dream guy. He has the looks, the smile, the moves, and the name to go with it all. He was positively my dream guy until he wasn't. I was almost Thad's bride, until I wasn't.

He was leading me down my path to my "Happily Ever After" life, until he wasn't. It was like my entire life just stopped. As I remember, those feelings of nothingness start to take over my being. Those tears that need to be shed can't come. *"Big Girls Don't Cry!"*

***

The next morning, I debate whether to finish the exposition or just go home. With my poor choice of partaking of three glasses of wine the night before my mind wasn't firing on all cylinders allowing for the best decisions to be made. From the business side of thoughts, there clearly were other exhibits I wanted to see but was it worth the risk of running into Thad, Roger and Brian? One part of me wanted to come face to face with them, hand them my business card as a way of saying, "See me now!" But the other part of me wanted to bypass the entire happening, run home and hide (and cry). *"Big Girls Don't Cry!"*

After spending half of the morning debating with

myself, I wander into the exhibit halls. I start at the opposite side of the venue from where I saw Brian, Roger and Thad the day before. As I was viewing brochures on pump jacks, I feel a tap on my shoulder. I turn around to gaze into a pair of very familiar hazel-colored eyes. Not to mention, seeing gorgeous brown wavy hair, plaid suit and tie and of course the signature monogrammed initials on a French cuff shirt with cuff links.

"Hello, Thad. What a surprise seeing you here all the way from Alaska!"

"Yes, it is a surprise seeing you as well. The company wants me to stay current with operation techniques that can be used in the frozen lands of Alaska."

"I see."

"So, what brings you to the expo?"

Thinking quickly, I pull out my business card proudly displaying my corporation name and logo. I mimic in reply, "I want to make sure I stay current with operation techniques for my company, KT Exploration,

Inc." Immediately, I see the chauvinistic look I see on the male faces of the oil and gas industry when they realize a female has her own oil and gas corporation.

"Well, I guess congratulations are in order. Let me take you to dinner tomorrow night after the expo and we can celebrate your company."

Every alarm starts blaring in my mind. I see red flags waving in my mind's eye. I can read "Danger Zone" signs all the way to the exit doors. But what do I do? I respond, "Sure."

"Great. I know a wonderful restaurant not far from the expo that serves a delicious Bananas Foster. I will text you the address. I will make reservations for 7:00. Got to run."

As I stand in the middle of the exhibit hall with my gaping mouth, I am trying to make sense of the last three minutes. Did I hear "Bananas Foster?" Did I say "Yes," again?

***

Feeling slightly ill, remembering I didn't eat breakfast because I was running late having wasted half the morning mulling over failed relationships, I step into a little café just outside the expo. I order my regular black coffee. Starting out on the rigs years before my use for coffee was to stay awake. I learned to drink coffee however it was brewed and for however long it had been sitting in the pot. I started to order a pastry but the words "Bananas Foster" filtered through my mind again. I felt faint. As I grab the counter to keep from falling, I feel familiar arms hug my waist. My head is swimming yet I make out a beautiful pair of bluer than blue eyes. I hear myself say, "Roger" as I fall unconscious in his arms.

I don't know how much time has passed as I slowly open my eyes but I quickly want to close them again. *Yikes!* I find myself in Roger's arms staring into his blue eyes. *What happened?* As Roger helps me to my feet, legs still wobbling, I am looking into his eyes once more. *Wow, why do his eyes send me to the moon and back?*

I can't even begin to think of the embarrassment I caused myself while unconscious. *Just don't think about it.* Somehow, I manage to gather myself and say, "Thank you for softening my fall. You seemed to be at the right place at the right time." *Oh, why did I say that? Can I have those words back?* Of course, he smiles that Roger smile with those gleaming eyes and responds, "Happy to be of service." *Really?* I am thinking will this moment ever end. I dust myself off being thankful I didn't fall out with my cup of coffee in hand. Forget the coffee, forget the pastry. I am out of here.

I turn to leave. Roger gently takes my hand and says, "It is great to see you again. How have you been?" *Great to see you again. How have you been? You talk about lame.*

"I have been fine." *No thanks to you.*

Again, I turn to leave. Roger, still holding my hand says, "Please, sit and talk." *Talk, talk about what:*

how you vanished out of my life, how you stole my childhood song...

I pull my hand out from his and I replace it with my business card. I bid Roger good-bye and practically run back into the expo to hopefully get lost in the crowd.

***

About the time I am wondering if this day can get any worse, I see Brian walking straight towards me. And yes, he is looking right at me, waving. He is upon me in an instant with a hug, kiss on the cheek saying, "Wow, it is great to see you. It has been too long." *Too long or not long enough. At this point, I am not sure.* I feebly respond, "Nice to see you, too." I point to his name tag. "I see you didn't follow your engineering endeavors after all."

"No, I went the accountant route."

"Are you happy with that path. I remember you were so passionate about engineering. We had even spoke of starting our own company one day."

"Well, my family's business needed more accounting help than engineering help. So, as you can see, I am the company's senior accountant," as he points to his name tag.

"I see." *I am not really up for small talk. I just want to disappear.*

"How about grabbing a sandwich with me. Everyone at the expo is breaking for lunch."

I was just about to agree when Brian added, "Like we did in college taking our study breaks." I put the skids on. I am not going down this path again. I hand him a business card saying, "I have work to do. Bye!" I walked as fast as I could to the nearest exit door. I took a quick peek back. Brian hasn't taken a step. He just keeps looking at my business card. I guess I gave him a shock. *Not half the shock he gave me years ago as he ended our relationship.*

***

Hours later, sitting in my room, I begin

contemplating this day, then the days, months, and years leading up to this day. So much time spent building relationships for them to only fall apart taking a huge chunk of me with the fall. I know I need to focus on where I went right along the way but the hurt inside brings me to remember all the wrongs that happened. *Have I become as bitter as I sounded speaking to Thad, Roger and Brian today?*

I feel my heart sinking as I think of Brian, my first love, my true love. I know we could have been together forever. My modest decision thinking we could have built a successful company as we shared endless fun along the way. Could haves, should haves…. He chose his family and business, not me.

I feel even more loss as Roger enters my mind. My brief encounter of "love hopes" only to find out I totally misjudged his character. I truly enjoyed sharing our work and play. I felt we met each other's needs. I guess not. He chose his success at my expense.

I feel my heart plummet thinking of Thad. My slight action brought me within 45 days of being his bride. How could I not see. Is love that blind? He chose his career instead of me.

***

During the last day of the expo, Thad sent a text with the address of the restaurant and a short message saying, "Looking forward to our celebration." A few hours later, Roger sends a text inviting me to dinner. I wonder how he got my phone number. Then, I remember, my phone number is on my business card I gave him. *Ugh!* I got a wild hair thinking well if Thad wants to celebrate, let's celebrate. I sent Roger a return message with the address of the restaurant Thad had reserved and added, "Meet you there at 7:00. Ask for the celebration table." Then, of course, I get a text from Brian. He too took the liberty to send a dinner invitation seeing my phone number on my business card. Now, I am out of control but I like it. I return the text message to

Brian sharing the same restaurant address and say, "See you at 7:00. Ask for the celebration table." *What a celebration this is going to be!*

***

Leaving the expo early, I took a few hours to find the perfect dress, shoes, handbag, the works. I couldn't wait for 7:00 to arrive. *Or could I, should I?* As they say, the time has come, the moment has arrived. Getting to the restaurant early, I ask the maître d' if I can stay hidden for a while. I shared that three friends were to arrive at 7:00 asking for the "Celebration Table" and would he please seat them together. As I peek through the kitchen window, I see Thad arrive, then Roger, then Brian. The maître d' ushers them all to the same table. Their faces were filled with bewilderment. I thought this is my "grand entrance time."

I begin with, "Hello, Thad, Roger, Brian. I don't believe you know each other so let me introduce you." After the introductions, I continue with, "You all have something in common, Me." Let me clarify my statement, "You all had something in common, Me." As I watch their eyes drop and their mouths open with shame and awkwardness, I feel a sense of reward and closure as I carry-on. Years ago, Brian you were my first love. We planned our futures together, forever. Yet you chose to walk away from our dreams and from me.

Roger, I thought you and I would create a lifestyle like no other couple. We had our work, our play. We had each other until you chose to totally dismiss our relationship once you got what you wanted, my song. I sure this will be news for you but, I had a double copyright on my song that superseded any behind-the-back shenanigans you thought you were pulling with your melody. The song has been revised and all proceeds go to a children's charity I have chosen.

Saving the best for last, Thad. I was your Bride-To-Be, your Happily Ever After. We were the perfect couple. I was head-over-heels in love as I thought you were too. I should have guessed with a name like Thaddeus Lee Baxter, III you would choose fame and more fortune over love.

With every word of love and truth, I feel tears streaming down my cheeks. *"Big Girls Don't Cry, Until They Do."* Having Thad's, Roger's and Brian's full attention watching my tears of years of heartbreak and hurt beyond imagine pouring out of me but now being transformed into tears of sadness and loss for them. "These tears are not shed for me, they are shed for you, Thad; for you, Roger; for you, Brian. When you said goodbye to me you said good-bye to a love like no other, to a life like no other, to a beautiful world full of hopes and dreams. When you said goodbye to me, I see now it is your loss and my gain."

As I walk out of the restaurant, looking back seeing looks of astonishment, I say, "Your meals are compliments of KT Exploration, Inc., so enjoy, especially the Bananas Foster. I hear it is the best."

I cried my river of tears to the oceans of each. Now, I step away from my tears of remorse in exchange for tears of happiness, happiness for me. And yes, "Big Girls Do Cry, Until They Don't." I am a "Big Girl." I always have been. I just had to believe in "Me."

I decide it is time to go forward as difficult as it may seem. But I encourage myself saying, "There are new adventures ahead beyond a modest decision, brief encounter and a slight action. There are great decisions to be made, long lasting relationships to embrace and major achievements to accomplish."

ACKNOWLEDGMENTS

The Engineering Programs at my alma mater, Texas A&M University. Thank you for preparing me for the "tasks at hand" from day one in the workplace, offshore, onshore, office or wherever my skills were needed. I am so proud to be an Aggie Women Legacy Award Recipient.

My "critique group" encouraging and supporting me through this writing journey.

My newest friend and graphic designer, Elizabeth Ashcroft. Thank you for helping me and Goodwin Global Publishing, LLC make this happen.

ABOUT THE AUTHOR

Renee Goodwin is an award-winning author/publisher of GG Life Lesson Storybook Series ® books. Renee has an undying passion for education which began at an early age. Through the years Renee has become an accomplished teacher, engineer, businesswoman, author and artist.

Renee is the recipient of the 2021 Texas A&M University Aggie Women Legacy award. She continues her legacy with her GG Life Lesson Storybook Series ® books on exhibit at the Cushing Library at Texas A&M University, showcased internationally and nationally at prominent book fairs and presented in the 2025 New York Times Book Review.

Renee is a 2025 Marquis Who's Who Biographical Honoree and Distinguished Leader featured in the Wall Street Journal. Renee is the International Association of Top Professionals (IAOTP) Top Children's Author of the Year 2025 and featured in the third edition of IAOTP's Top 25 Global Impact Leaders Publication.

Renee created her own publishing company, Goodwin Global Publishing, LLC providing authors professional contract publishing services, producing quality products, while establishing loyal and long-term relationships.

Renee offers GG Life Lesson Storybook Series ® books and her novels for purchase on her website, personally autographed and mailed to you (www.ggstorybooks.com).

Renee is happy to announce her most recent novel, Big Girls Don't Cry – Until They Do. You can read more about Renee, her children's books and novels on her author page on Goodwin Global Publishing website (www.goodwinglobalpublishing.com).